P9-ASC-881

# MOBY DICK

Treasury of Illustrated Classics™

# MOBY DICK

*by*

**Herman Melville**

**Abridged, adapted, and illustrated**

*by*

quadrum■

Kappa Books Publishers, LLC.

Cover art by Quadrum



Printed in U.S.A.

# Contents

CHAPTER 1

# Love of Water

Call me Ishmael. Some years ago, having little money in my purse, and nothing to interest me onshore, I thought I'd sail a bit and see the watery world. I decided to go to sea each and every time I got depressed and miserable on land.

The city of the Manhattoes is bordered by wharves and coral reefs. Right and left, the streets take you toward the water. One can see people gazing at the water there. Walk around the city

and what do you see? Posted like silent soldiers all around the town stand thousands of men fixed in ocean dreams. Some leaning against the spiels; some seated upon the pier heads; some looking at the bulwarks of ships from China. But these are all landsmen, all tied down to their boring, dull jobs. Is there no hope for them? They want to get as close to the water as they can without falling in, and there they stand, inlanders all of them. They come from lanes and alleys, streets and avenues. But they stand here, united. Some sort of magic makes the most absentminded of men be pulled toward his dreams of water.

Now, when I say that I go out to sea whenever I feel miserable, it may not necessarily be as a passenger. To be a passenger, you need money in your purse. Besides, passengers get seasick, grow quarrelsome, don't sleep at night, and do not enjoy themselves much. So, I never go as a passenger; nor do I ever go to sea as a commodore, or a captain, or a cook. I leave all those things to men who like them.

When I go out to sea, I go as a simple sailor, right before the mast. True, I'm given orders and made to jump from

one place to another like a grasshopper. It's irritating at first. The transition is a difficult one, I assure you, from a schoolmaster to a sailor—it requires a strong mind to enable you to grin and bear it. But it gets easier over time. So what if some old captain orders me to sweep the entire deck to and fro? I don't think that is insulting. Who isn't a slave in one way or another?

Well, then, however the old sea captains may order me about—however they may thump and punch me about—I have the satisfaction of knowing that it is all right; that everybody else has one way or another served in much the same way.

Another reason I go as a sailor is because the sea captains make it a point to pay me for my trouble. They don't pay passengers, now, do they? No, it's always the other way: Passengers pay. There's a big difference in paying and being paid!

And finally, I want to go as a sailor because of the wholesome experience and the breath of pure air from the forecastle deck. The commodore on the quarterdeck thinks he's breathing fresh air, not knowing that it is secondhanded by those on the forecastle deck.

I decided that instead of going as a merchant sailor as usual, this time I would go on a whaling trip. My fate would come with me as my guard. My main reason for wanting to go whaling is the whale itself. Such a huge and mysterious monster—swimming in his massive bulk under wild and distant seas—has raised my curiosity! Other men may not have been interested by this, but for me, I love to sail the forbidden seas. I itch for anything that's far away. So I welcomed the whaling voyage.

CHAPTER 2

# The Spouter Inn

I filled my carpetbag with a shirt or two and left my hometown, Manhatto, New York, for Nantucket. Nantucket was the place for whaling. I had two days to spare, so I went off to find somewhere to stay till then. After coming upon various inns and rejecting them duly, I came across a swinging sign over a door, painted in white, with what looked like a jet of water surging upward. The words The Spouter Inn—Peter Coffin were written on it. The house was

shabby and dilapidated looking. For some reason, I decided to give it a try.

The first thing I saw when I entered the inn was a horrible picture of a sinking ship and a whale. On the opposite wall were all sorts of scary weapons, each meant for killing or capturing whales. There were clubs, spears, whaling lances, and rusty harpoons. But each weapon carried a story of its attack on a whale. The place was filled with young seamen. I walked up to the landlord and asked for a room only to be told that there was no room available.

"But you wouldn't mind sharing your blanket with a harpooner, would you? Since you're going whaling, you might as well get used to it!" said the landlord. I wasn't comfortable sharing my bed with another person, but I chose that over wandering aimlessly in a strange town during the night.

"Sit down, then," said the landlord, grinning. "You're probably hungry. Supper will be ready soon."

All throughout supper, I watched out for the harpooner. When a fellow in a green coat walked in and greeted his comrades in a lewd fashion, I asked, "Landlord, that isn't the harpooner, is it?"

"No," he replied, "the harpooner is dark complexioned. He'll be here soon."

I watched the door nervously for my roommate to appear. It was after midnight when I turned to my landlord

*Moby Dick*

and said, "Landlord, where is the fellow? Does he always go to sleep late?"

"Not really. He's an 'early to bed, early to rise' sort of a fellow. I'm guessing he's peddling tonight. Must be having trouble selling his head."

"His what?" I gasped.

"Relax," said the landlord. "The harpooner has arrived from the South Seas with a lot of shrunken heads from New Zealand. Great curios, if I may say so. He's sold all but one. I told him not to go out trying to sell it tomorrow, since a lot of good people go to church."

"That man sounds quite dangerous," I said.

"He pays regularly, so who am I to complain?" replied the landlord. "It's getting late, so I'll take you to your room."

There were exactly four pieces of furniture in the room: an old sea chest, a wooden chair, a rough shelf, and a

bed big enough to fit four harpooners! A tall harpoon stood at the head of the bed, and a seaman's bag lay on the floor. I quickly undressed myself, blew out the light, and fell into bed. I didn't sleep for a long while; I kept tossing and turning. Finally, I managed to doze off. Soon after, I woke up hearing heavy footsteps outside the room. I rolled over and saw light coming from under the door.

Must be that harpooner! I thought.

Holding the light in one hand and the shrunken head in the other, the stranger entered the room. I watched him stuff that head inside his bag. He turned, and the shock vibrated through my body. What a face! It was a dark purplish color, covered with black squares all over. He took off his hat, and I stifled a cry of surprise. He was bald except for a lock of hair that grew in the center of his head.

He had twisted that lock into a knot. His head looked like a mildewed skull. He fumbled with his bag for a bit and pulled out a tomahawk pipe.

Had the man been standing before me while I ate my dinner, I'd have bolted faster than a rabbit! As he undressed, I saw that his body was covered with black squares. He walked over to where he hung his coat and took out a tiny hunchbacked idol of sorts, a handful of wood shavings, a candle, and a few ship biscuits. He lit the fire, burned the biscuits, and made an offering to the figure. As he worshipped the idol, I continued to watch, transfixed, as he chanted. Once he was done, he shoved the idol back into his coat pocket roughly.

Suddenly, he picked up his tomahawk and examined the head for a second. He popped it open and puffed out a huge cloud of tobacco smoke. He then jumped into bed, tomahawk between his teeth. I shouted and scrambled back to the corner of the bed.

"Who the devil are you?" yelled the harpooner. "Speak, or I'll kill you!" He spread ashes all over the bed, and I thought he was going to burn me alive. Luckily, at that moment, the landlord appeared at the door with a light in his hand. I ran to him in relief.

"Don't worry now!" grinned the landlord. "Queequeg won't hurt a hair on your head."

"Why didn't you tell me that your harpooner is a cannibal?" I roared.

"I thought you'd figured it out when I said he'd be peddling heads all over town. Go back to sleep, now. Queequeg, this man sleep you—you sabbee?" the landlord said, trying to imitate Queequeg's dialect.

"Me sabbee," Queequeg grunted, and began smoking his pipe.

He politely motioned for me to get back to bed.

"Landlord, please tell him that I'll stay here, if he stops smoking his pipe in bed. I'm not insured yet! Good night."

Queequeg got into bed and rolled over to the far side. I got into bed and slept like a baby.

CHAPTER 3

# A Good Friend

When I woke up the next morning, I found Queequeg's arm wrapped around me like he was sleeping with his wife! Very uncomfortable with that thought, I poked him awake. He grunted, threw away his arm, and sat, stiffly looking at me. He stood, stretched, and courteously gestured that he'd change first and leave the room so that I might change comfortably. I felt guilty for being rude while he was so polite.

He put on his tall beaver hat and then his boots. He put on his pants, then shrugged into his shirt. Next, he took a wet piece of soap and began lathering his face. I wondered what he'd use to shave, when he walked over to the harpoon and removed its head. He sharpened it on his boot and began scraping his cheeks with it. I was quite amazed by his morning rituals! Once he was ready, he proudly marched out of the room.

During breakfast, I was surprised to see that those at the table were quiet. I honestly expected a loud, boisterous group of sailors exchanging seafaring stories. Instead, I found a table full of whalemen, from chief mates to harpooners to ship keepers, silently eating.

After breakfast, I found myself alone in the public room with Queequeg. I saw him lift a heavy book and go through it in his strange language. He whistled after counting every fifty pages. As I saw him, I realized that he didn't mingle with the other sailors. Here was a man who was twenty thousand miles away from home in a place as foreign to him as the planet Jupiter. Yet he was always at ease with himself, so I felt myself drawn to him. I tried to talk to him. When he asked if I would be sharing the room tonight as well, I said yes. He looked pleased.

I took the book he was holding and tried to explain it to him—what the printing meant and what the pictures described. I soon engaged his interest. We managed to talk about the different sites in town and even shared a social smoke between us, with him passing his pipe to me and me back to him. We sat there puffing the pipe in companionable silence.

After our smoke, he clasped his hands

around my waist, pressed his forehead against mine, and said that we were married; which in his country's terms meant that we were friends for life. I felt a bit awkward at that, since here in America, we don't trust people that easily.

After another friendly smoke and supper, we went back to the room. He gave the shrunken head to me as a gift. He rummaged under his bag and took out thirty dollars in silver, which he promptly divided in half, saying one half was mine. I refused, obviously, but he picked up the change and forced it in my pocket. He then took out the hunchback idol and motioned for me to come join him in worshipping it. Therein lay the problem. As I was a good Christian, I knew that idol worship was against my religion.

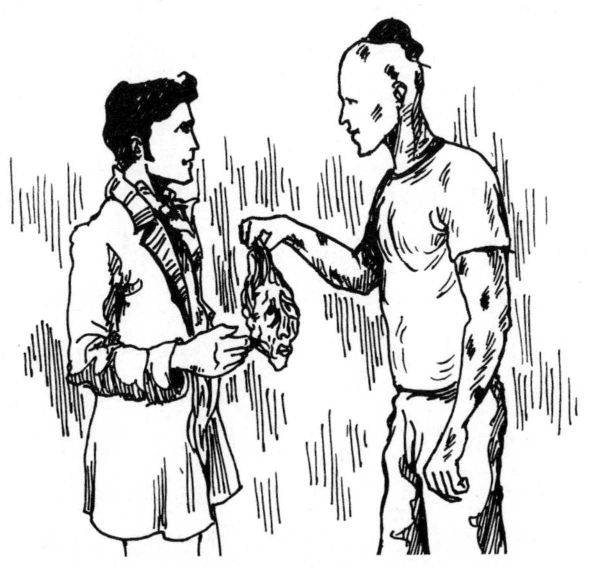

Then, I wondered why God would be jealous of a piece of wood. So I lit the fire, burned the biscuit and offered it to the idol, bowed down once or twice, and went to bed.

The next morning, Queequeg told me all about himself.

"Queequeg born in Kokovoko, small-ee island in South Pacific," he started. "Queequeg father, king; his uncle high priest. Queequeg become king after old father dies. But Queequeg have to see Christian world first and bring back great improvements to his people."

Apparently, when a Sag Harbor ship visited his father's bay, Queequeg begged the captain to allow him passage to the New World. But because the ship was full already with crew members, he wasn't allowed on board. The captain denied his request, so Queequeg took his canoe and paddled to a distant strait, one he knew the ship must pass through once she left the island.

Once there, he waited silently until the ship glided smoothly through the strait. He jumped to the side of the boat and vaulted himself over the ship's rail. The captain tried in vain to throw him overboard and even whipped him with a cutlass, but Queequeg didn't budge. The captain finally relented. He told Queequeg to make himself at home, even though this young prince never even saw the captain's cabin. He was put with the sailors and was made into a whaleman. He told me that he wanted to learn the practices from the Christians, arts to make his people happier than they already were. But, alas! The practices of whalemen soon convinced him that Christian men could be quite miserable and cruel, more so than his father's heathens.

Being someone who idolizes others, he continued to live with them, dress like them, and even talk like them. I asked him indirectly if he'd stayed away from home long enough that it was time to head back. His father might be dead or near to being that now. He told me he didn't want to go back yet; he wanted to go out to sea. Hearing this, I told him my plans of whaling and sailing out of Nantucket. He immediately decided to accompany me on my voyage so that he could share every aspect of it with me.

His story ended with the pipe's last puff. He embraced me, pressed his forehead against mine, blew out the light, and went back to sleep again.

*Moby Dick*

CHAPTER 4

# Queequeg the Hero

The next morning, Queequeg and I brought a wheelbarrow to take things out to the dock. He told me about the first time he had seen a wheelbarrow. Not knowing its purpose, he strapped his sea chest to it and carried the wheelbarrow on his back.

"People must've laughed at you!" I told him.

"Different people laugh-ee in different ways," he said. "Another story. Sea captain visiting Kokovoko Island. He be

tell-ee to come to wedding of Queequeg sister. High priest take big bowl and dip fingers in coconut juice to bless before give-ee to guests. Captain not sabbee. Him wash-ee hands in juice. What you tink now? That Queequeg people not laugh?"

"Well, I suppose they did," I admitted.

We'd arrived at the Moss, a small ship sailing from New Bedford to Nantucket. We were boarding the ship when some of the passengers began pointing fingers at Queequeg and making fun of

him. One particular jab got him angry. So Queequeg dropped his harpoon, lifted the rude fellow, and threw him in the air.

Afterward, the fellow complained to the captain, who came out thundering, "What the devil did you mean by that? You could've killed him!"

"What say him?" asked Queequeg.

"Captain say that you almost kill-ee that man there," I said, pointing to the shivering man.

Queequeg snorted in contempt. "That man is small-ee fish. I no kill-ee. I go kill-ee big whale!"

"If you try any more tricks, I'll kill-ee you!" roared the captain.

Just then something happened while the mainsail was being raised. The boom, or long pole that stretches the sails, was now swinging from one side to another. In one swish, it pushed the rude man overboard and continued

# *Moby Dick*

to swing wildly back and forth. People stood there, paralyzed with shock, not knowing what to do. All except Queequeg. He got to his knees and crawled under the swinging boom to a rope. He tied one end of the rope to the bulwarks and flung the other like a lasso over the rail. He then took his shirt and jacket off and dived perfectly into the freezing water. For a minute we didn't see anyone but Queequeg swimming around. Suddenly, he disappeared under the water, only to resurface a moment later, dragging a limp figure behind him. The man who had insulted Queequeg was saved by him, and the captain apologized to Queequeg. I decided to stick to my best friend like a barnacle.

*Moby Dick*

CHAPTER 5

# Who is Captain Ahab?

I had to part with Queequeg for a short while when we arrived at Nantucket. Back in our room at the Spouter Inn, Queequeg had given me his wooden idol; it was called Yojo. This was a sign that I alone was to pick out the ship for us to sign up with. After observing various ships, I finally settled on the Pequod, a small, old-fashioned vessel. I met a suntanned, wrinkled gentleman on board and told him that I wanted to sign up. He

introduced himself as Captain Peleg, one of the two owners of the Pequod.

"Why do you want to go whaling?" he asked me. "I'd like to know before I take you on."

"I'd like to see what whaling is, sir."

"Have you seen Captain Ahab?"

"Captain Ahab?"

"The captain of this ship. Why don't you have a good look at him before you get into this whaling business? You'll find him easily enough. He's got only one leg."

"He lost the other while whaling, then?" I asked.

"Lost it! It was bitten off by the biggest monster to ever swim these waters!"

I was relentless and finally persuaded Captain Peleg that I wanted to sign up. I also mentioned Queequeg, whom the captain said to bring along as well.

As I was leaving the ship, I realized that I hadn't seen Captain Ahab yet.

"Where can I find him?" I asked.

"Who?" asked Captain Peleg.

"Captain Ahab."

"Why do you want to see him? You've been signed up already."

"Yes, but I would still like to see him."

"Don't count on it," he replied. "He's

not too well. He doesn't even see me often, and I doubt he'll see you. Good man, though, he is. Named after a king in the Bible."

"Wasn't the biblical Ahab wicked and wasn't he killed?" I asked.

"Shh! Don't say that on board ever! I know the captain. He may have lost his mind a little on his last trip home, but you can't really blame him considering a whale bit his leg off! Don't judge him by that wicked name. He didn't choose it. He's got a young wife and son, you know."

I went back to Queequeg, thinking about the mysterious Captain Ahab.

CHAPTER 6

# Queequeg's Mark

As Queequeg and I were boarding the ship, Captain Peleg's gruff voice stopped us.

"Oye! Who's that with you?"

"My friend, Queequeg, the one I told you would be joining me," I replied.

"You didn't tell me he's a cannibal! I don't allow pagans on my ship unless they're reformed by the church. Where are his papers?"

"Why would he need the papers? He's a member of the First Congregational

Church," I said.

"How long has he been a member? Not for long, I reckon, young man. He hasn't been baptized properly, either," said Captain Peleg. "Had he been baptized, he'd have gotten those colors off his face," he grunted.

"Listen," I said, "he's a born member, and a deacon himself."

"Come on," said the captain. "What church are you talking about?"

Feeling pushed, I said, "The First Congregational Church of the World—the church that you and I and every other person worships in. We all belong to that church. We have small differences, but in the one grand belief in God, we join hands."

"Blimey! That's the best sermon I've heard in ages!" said the captain. "Maybe you should join on as a missionary. Tell me, has your friend ever stuck a fish?"

Queequeg understood the question and quickly jumped onto one of the lifeboats hanging on the side. He took out the harpoon and aimed it at the

water.

"Cap'n! You see that small-ee tar water? Well, suppose that isn't small-ee tar but big-ee whale's eye. . ."

Pulling his hand back, he threw the harpoon into the water and struck the tar clear out of sight.

"Now," said Queequeg as he reeled in his harpoon, "suppose that was big-ee whale's eye, big-ee whale be dead."

Captain Peleg wasted no time in signing on Queequeg. A while later, Queequeg and I left the Pequod to walk around town for a bit. Suddenly we were stopped by a stranger who was shabbily dressed and had spots on his face.

"Have you signed up for her then?" he asked us, pointing at the Pequod.

"We have," I replied.

"Is there anything in those papers about your souls?"

"Our what?" I asked him.

"I guess you don't have any souls." He shrugged, then continued: "But Old Thunder's got enough for the other fellows on board!"

"Who's Old Thunder?" I wondered.

"Captain Ahab. He's the captain of your ship."

Well, now! "I've heard he's a good captain," I defended.

"True, but what about the other things?" the stranger asked.

"Listen to me," I said. "All I know about the captain is that he's got only one leg. Now if there's something more important to tell us, then out with it—or else be gone!"

"Well said, lad! I like a man who speaks up. You're just the man for him. I'll bid you good day now!"

"Look here, man. I know you're keeping something from us. I can see it in your face! Out with it now!" I snapped.

"Good day, mates!" And, saying this, the stranger turned to walk away.

"Who are you?" I called out as he walked away.

"Elijah," he replied.

Shaking my head, I walked the other way with Queequeg, both of us agreeing that the old sailor was a fake. But we worried that the biblical Elijah was a prophet who predicted bad things. . . .

CHAPTER 7

# All Aboard!

We waited a few days while the Pequod was being loaded with supplies for a three-day journey. When the day finally came, we reached the docks at six o'clock in the morning. As we were about to board the ship, we heard a voice call out.

"Stop!" We turned to find Elijah holding us back.

"Don't go on that ship!" he hissed.

"We shall. Who are you to stop us?" I questioned.

"Have you even seen some of the men going toward this ship?"

"Yes, but it was too dim to see who they were," I replied.

"Too dim...oh well. Morning to ye both!" Saying this, the strange man left.

Feeling quite annoyed with that encounter, I boarded the ship. The Pequod soon lifted its anchor, and we set sail. The vessel was headed by Captain Peleg. When we were out of the bay and on the ocean, a small sailboat came to the ship to take Captain Peleg back to shore. Captain Ahab, I believe, had come on board the night before.

The chief mate of the ship was Starbuck,

a thin, steady man, who seemed like the brave, reliable sort. Having lost both his brother and father at sea, Starbuck wasn't a man to take unnecessary risks. The second mate was Stubb. He was an easygoing man, and also a chain-smoker. Flask was the third mate. The short, stubby man seemed like he was going whale hunting just for the fun of it!

Now, each of these three mates commanded their own small whaling boat. They each had their own harpooner selected by the mates themselves. Chief mate Starbuck chose Queequeg. Stubb chose Tashtego, a Native American who looked like a proud warrior-hunter. Third among the harpooners was Daggoo, a gigantic African. There was a large gold hoop in each of his ears. With the three mates taking command of the ship, Captain Ahab remained out of sight.

*Moby Dick*

CHAPTER 8

# Captain Ahab

A few days after we left Nantucket, we came on deck at the call of the afternoon watch. That was when I saw him. The man looked like a bronze statue, not a weak, ill man. A white scar threaded its way from his gray hair down his cheek and neck until it disappeared into his clothes. It looked like a line in a great tree when struck by lightning, but still alive and branded! One of his legs was made of ivory, carved from a smooth

bone from a whale's mouth. His firm posture amazed me. How could he stand on that leg like a statue on a rocking ship! Then, I realized why.

A half-inch hole had been drilled into either side of the officer's quarterdecks. He fitted his bone leg there, keeping him erect as he watched all that happened below on the decks. He looked quite disturbed at something unknown.

Captain Ahab came on deck more often as we moved southward and as we hit warmer weather. He'd either stand with his leg fixed or he'd sit on a stool fixed the same way. Sometimes, the restless movement of his wooden leg would keep us awake at night. Once, Stubb jokingly told the captain to cover his ivory leg should he feel like taking a walk in the night again. Ahab turned on him instantly, his eyes blazing fire.

"How dare you talk to me like that!

Down, dog, and to your kennel!" he thundered. At Ahab's rage, Stubb became speechless for a moment. He stared at Ahab, wide-eyed, but then very soon recovered himself.

"Sir, I'm not used to being spoken to in that way. I don't like it. I will not be called a dog."

"Then be called ten times a donkey and be gone!" Ahab cried, and shoved Stubb out of the way.

Stubb muttered to himself as he walked by the other men. "I don't know whether to pray for him or whether to strike him. He's barking mad! What can be troubling him so much that he stays in bed only three hours a day? Even then he doesn't sleep. The steward says his pillows and sheets are rumpled and his bed is like a hot brick. He's full of mystery, that man."

One fine morning, after breakfast, Ahab's steady step was heard as usual.

The dents made from the steps of his ivory leg looked deeper than usual, as if he walked in nervousness or with a lot of tension. He had many lines in his forehead. All day he paced the deck back and forth, by the end of which, he stopped by the bulwarks and ordered Starbuck to send everybody aft. Starbuck was surprised at the order but hurried to call the men and tell them to assemble at the rear end of the ship.

Ahab looked at his crew. "What do you do when you see a whale?" he asked us.

"We sing to him," came the answer.

"Very good! What next?" Ahab demanded.

"We lower the whaling boats and go after it."

"By what tune do you men row your boats?"

" 'A Dead Whale or a Stove Boat'!"

Ahab's face broke into a huge grin

when the entire crew sang the chorus together. Then, he took out a coin and called for a hammer.

"Look here! This is a Spanish ounce of gold. Whosoever spots a white-headed whale with a wrinkled brow and a crooked jaw, with three holes punctured on his side, gets this coin!"

The crew cheered loudly at this chance to win a small piece of treasure. Ahab took the coin and, with a nail, hammered it to the mast.

"This whale is white," he declared. "Even if you see a bubble, sing out."

So far, the most interested of the crew were the three harpooners, Tashtego, Daggoo, and Queequeg. At the mention of a wrinkled brow, a memory came to each of them.

"Captain Ahab!" called out Tashtego. "Are you talking of the white whale named Moby Dick?"

"Aye, yes. You know him, man?"

"Does he move his tail before he goes underwater?" asked Tashtego.

"Does he have an odd spout and is he mighty quick, Captain?" asked Daggoo.

"And, Captain, he have two, three iron in him hide, too! All twist-ee like . . . like . . ." Queequeg circled his hand around and around.

"Corkscrew!" cried the captain. "That's right, Queequeg, the harpoons lie twisted inside him! Aye, Daggoo, his spout is a big one. Yes, Tashtego, he does move his tail from side to side before submerging. Death and devils, men! You've seen him! You've seen Moby Dick!"

"Captain Ahab," called Starbuck, "was it Moby Dick who took your leg off?"

"Aye, it was that very monster! I'll chase that whale all around the Cape of Good Hope and around Cape Horn

and around the flames of hell before I give up!" he cried. "That is what you've been shipped for, men. To help me find Moby Dick, and destroy him! What say you, men? Are you all brave enough to join hands with me on this hunt?"

The crew cheered their alliance with the captain to the point of deafness.

Ahab almost sobbed at his men's dedication.

"God bless you, men. Steward, go and fetch out the rum for the men!"

Amidst the cheers, he turned and saw Starbuck standing silently.

"What is it, mate? Are you not willing to chase Moby Dick?"

"I'm game for the chase and the hunt, Captain, but only because the profession calls for it. I signed up for the whaling part of it, not for my captain's revenge!" Starbuck was the only one who opposed the captain, but he didn't back down completely. "God save me, God save us all!" he muttered.

Captain Ahab went back to filling a large drinking mug with rum. "Drink and pass!" he cried. He handed the mug to the nearest seaman, who drank and passed it on to the one after him. This went on till the tumbler was almost empty and the captain

called out for a refill.

He then called for the three mates to step forward and said, “Cross your lances so that I may revive the noble customs of my ancestors.”

Gripping the three crossed lances at the center, he gazed deeply at each of his mates until they looked away, uncomfortable. “Down with your lances.” When the lances were lowered, Ahab turned to the three harpooners.

“Remove the blade from the pole, men.” The harpooners detached the iron tips and left their wooden poles with an opening on the top. Ahab filled up the poles with rum and told the harpooners to drink up.

“Drink and swear! Death to Moby Dick! Death to the White Whale!”

CHAPTER 9

# Moby Dick

With greedy ears, I heard the history of the White Whale who bit off my captain's leg; Moby Dick, the one whale all of us swore to hunt and kill, once spotted. I cried my oath and alliance to the captain, along with the rest of the crew. I soon began acquiring information about whales and whaling in general and of Moby Dick in particular.

Of all the whales, the sperm whale is the most valuable because of the white waxlike substance that is taken from the oil in the whale's head; it is used for making perfumes and for lighting lamps throughout the world.

It was only because Moby Dick was different from the others that he could easily be spotted from a distance. Not only did he have a white, wrinkled forehead and a large white hump, but also his whole body was colored white, earning him the nickname the White Whale.

He was known to swim away frantically at the sight of whaling boats. He'd let them chase him and, after a distance, he'd turn around and charge into them, either having them drive back to the main ship in fear or shatter their tiny vessels into pieces as he barged through. He once shattered three boats, and when the captain saw his men struggling for their lives in a swirling whirlpool made by Moby Dick's rapid

# *Moby Dick*

movements, he took out his knife and charged toward him like a madman. That captain was Captain Ahab. And it was at that moment that Moby Dick caught him by the leg and took it off! Ahab swore to take revenge and destroy that whale.

He felt that this whale in particular was God's most evil creation. Quite frankly, I was amazed at how he got the entire crew to hate Moby Dick as much as he did, as if Moby Dick had done them harm, too!

CHAPTER 10

# The Phantom Five

One moonlit night, we were standing on deck filling up a barrel with fresh water. Suddenly, one of the men whispered, “Oye, did you hear that?”

“Hear what?”

“That noise!”

“What noise?”

“There it went again. Came from the hatches, it did. It sounded like a cough.”

“Be quiet! It’s nothing but the soaked biscuits you ate that’s making all that noise from inside your stomach! Now hand me that bucket and get back to work."

"Grin all you want, you fool," spat the seaman. "We'll see what turns up. It came from below decks. I'm guessing the captain knows something about this as well. I heard Stubb tell Flask this morning!"

Everyone resumed their tasks for a bit. Just then, Tashtego, who was up in the crow's nest keeping watch, called out, "There she blows! There! There! There!"

"Where—away?"

"On the lee-beam, about two miles off! A school of them!"

The lee-beam was the side of the ship that was away from the wind. Instantly, there was a commotion on deck.

"Get me the exact time, Steward!

Quick! Quick!" cried Ahab. The steward, Dough-Boy, ran to the cabin, noted the exact time, and gave it to Ahab.

We knew he kept careful notes about his journeys and of various sightings. Three boats were lowered into the sea.

Suddenly, we heard a loud cry. Everyone took their eyes off the whales and turned to glare at Ahab, only to see him surrounded by five dusky phantoms that appeared out of nowhere!

These five phantoms began lowering one of the lifeboats silently and slowly.

"Fedallah, everything ready there?" called out Ahab.

"Ready!" came a hissed reply from a man wearing a turban that covered his long white hair and who had one tooth protruding evilly from his mouth. He wore a black jacket and pants. The others wore a traditional yellow costume that came from Manilla. This meant that they were a tribe from the Philippine Islands, near Australia. They were said to be quite superstitious.

"Lower away!" Ahab ordered.

The men jumped over the rail and onto the lowering boats. In the fourth boat that was being rowed by the five strangers stood Ahab.

"Starbuck! Stubb! Flask! Spread out! I want you to cover as much of the area as possible!" he yelled.

For a minute, when two boats touched each other, Stubb leaned out and asked Starbuck what he thought about the men in yellow.

"Those five were smuggled on board before the ship even sailed," said Starbuck. "Sad business, but it's all for the best."

"I thought so, too!" said Stubb. "No wonder he went down to the hold so often. Those men were hidden there. They're after the White Whale, too. Oh well, can't be helped. Fall back, men! We aren't after the White Whale today!"

Moby Dick

CHAPTER 11

# After the First Lowering

I remembered the mysterious shadows creeping aboard the ship in the dim Nantucket dawn. I also remember the puzzling hints Elijah gave us.

Meanwhile, Ahab, who was out of our hearing range, went much ahead of the other boats. The five men in yellow worked like machines. They looked like steel. In smooth movements they rose and fell against the motion of their boat, and they moved their oars through the water in a singular stroke, as well! The man, Fedallah, had stripped off his jacket and was sitting bare-chested. He was pulling the harpooner's oar, while on the other end, Ahab was steadily managing the steering oar. The whales had settled down into the waters. From his place, Ahab saw this clearly when the others couldn't.

"Every man look out along his oar!" Ahab shouted. "Stand up and brace yourself, Queequeg!"

The harpooner gracefully jumped on the triangular raised box on the bow and eagerly looked at the spot where the chase was last described. Even Starbuck braced himself, keeping a steely gaze on the deep blue waters. Not very far away, Flask's boat was also lying breathlessly still, its commander standing recklessly on top of the loggerhead.

Suddenly, the air changed and the water vibrated and rumbled. All four boats were then in full pursuit of that one spot of quivering water and air. Beneath these waters, whales were swimming, and the spouts of water that they gave out were a dead giveaway.

"Pull, my good men, pull!" whispered Starbuck softly yet intensely. His command was different from Flask's and Stubb's as they shouted out their commands. It was truly a sight to see the four boats battling through the

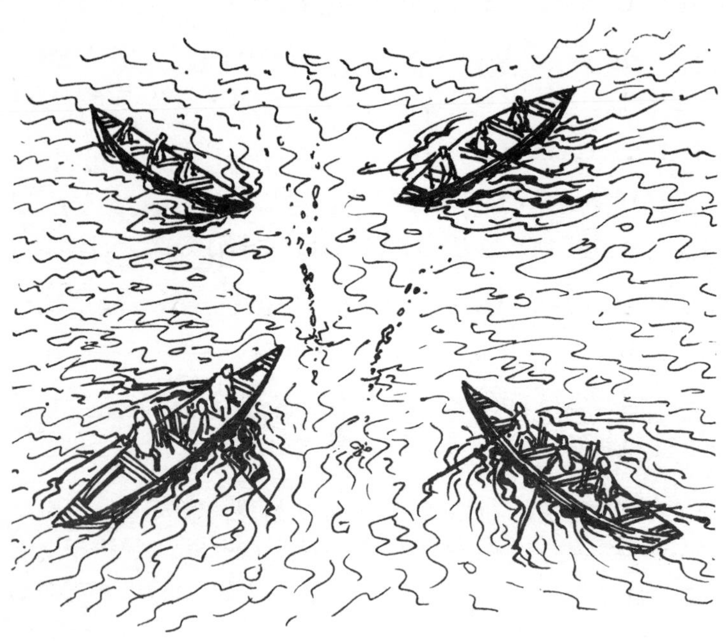

waves, going up and down them like sleds. This was coupled with the cries of the oarsmen as they struggled to keep their oars and boats steady. The Pequod bore down on the boats with her sails wide open and stretched like a worried mother going after her children!

Starbuck and his men were now after

three whales, and our boat rushed along in the rising wind and mist. Starbuck turned to Queequeg and said, "Stand up!"

Queequeg stood up and braced himself. He waited until Starbuck said, "That's his hump. There, there! Give it to him!"

The harpoon thrown by Queequeg cut through the air with a whoosh! And then, the confusion began. There seemed to be an invisible push coming from behind us while from the front, we seemed to be hitting a hard wall of sorts. The sail collapsed and exploded; a gush of hot vapor came up near us. Something rolled and tumbled like an earthquake beneath us.

The whole crew was half-suffocated and nauseated as they were being tossed from one place to another. It was a mad mixture of waves, whale, and harpoon, in which the whale,

barely nicked by the harpoon, escaped.

Our boat was separated from the others. We couldn't even call out to them, and they wouldn't have heard us anyway in this storm. The Pequod couldn't be seen in the thick mist. As dawn came, we sat there, completely drenched and shivering, with no hope at all.

Suddenly, Queequeg jumped to his feet and cupped his hand to his ear, as if listening for something. We started concentrating, too. That's when we heard it. A faint creaking! Before we could blink, the Pequod cut through the mist and came bearing down on us! We managed to jump into the sea, seconds before the boat was crushed under the Pequod. We swam about like fishes, fighting against the waves until the Pequod safely picked us up. We found out that the other three boats had gotten back just in time. We stood on the deck like drowned rats.

"Queequeg," I said, shaking the water off me, "does this happen often, my friend?"

He nodded, as did Stubbs and Flask, who were with us. Since all of them obviously thought that what had passed was quite normal when out whaling, there was only one thing left for me to do.

"Come downstairs with me, Queequeg," I said. "I want you to be a witness, my lawyer, and adviser. I'm going to make a rough draft of my will."

CHAPTER 12

# The Albatross

We soon began to sail along the Cape of Good Hope. Not the best name in the world to give the place, for it gives you anything but hope! That place should be called Cape Tormentoto because its wild and rough waves do nothing but torment you. It was in this place that we came across another ship battling the howling winds and the sprays of water thrown by the waves. It was the Albatross, a ship that hadn't seen home in God alone knows

how long. The craft was bleached like the skeleton of a stranded walrus. Her sides were traced with reddened rust. Only her lower sails were in place. She was a wild sight. There were three long-bearded men aboard who seemed to be dressed in animal skin. The ship looked shabby and worn out, having survived the seas over the last couple of years.

"Ship ahoy!" Ahab called out to the captain of the Albatross. "Have you seen the White Whale?"

But the strange captain, leaning over the bulwarks, was putting the trumpet to his mouth to reply when it slipped from his grasp and fell into the sea. In

spite of the rising wind, he tried yelling out his reply, but in vain. His ship was moving forward slowly but steadily. The crew aboard the Pequod realized that this was the first time the White Whale was mentioned to anyone apart from their ship. Captain Ahab knew that as the wind was blowing from behind him, his voice would get carried better to the Albatross. He picked up his trumpet and yelled, "Ship, ahoy! This is the Pequod! When you get home, tell them to forward all letters to the Pacific Ocean. And if I'm not back three years from now, tell them to send the letters to . . ."

By then, the ship had sailed past them and out of hearing distance.

"Swim away from me, why don't you," muttered Ahab as he watched the Albatross sail toward home while they sailed farther away from it.

Moby Dick

CHAPTER 13

# The Town-Ho

Not long after, we passed another ship, called the Town-Ho. This time, Ahab allowed them to visit us. A few of the crew members came aboard our ship. They whispered some of their secrets to Tashtego and left soon after. When he told us what they had told him, we were filled with even more curiosity and interest about Moby Dick.

An officer and a sailor got into a heated argument over an unfair order to sweep the deck of the Town-Ho. In anger, the

sailor knocked the officer out and the others got involved as well, causing a mutiny.

Steelkilt, a sailor, was about to kill Radney, the chief mate, when someone caught sight of Moby Dick. Radney's boat was the first to be lowered away.

As Radney stood, spear in hand, he was washed overboard. Moby Dick caught him between his jaws, reared up, and plunged into the water. When the whale rose again, he had pieces of Radney's shirt in his mouth. The rest of the crew chased the whale, but he managed to disappear.

Hearing this story put Moby Dick in all our minds. At that moment, Daggoo, who was keeping watch, saw a great white mass floating up and down.

"There she goes! The White Whale is up ahead!"

Ahab shouted out commands to lower the boats. I watched with interest as a large, colored mass hundreds of yards long, floated by us. It had countless arms coming from its center swirling and twirling around the water like snakes. It looked more or less like a ghost. It disappeared, making a loud sucking sound.

Starbuck was taking in slow breaths. "I'd rather fight with Moby Dick than see that ghost again!"

"What was it, sir?" asked Flask.

"That was a giant squid. It is said that very few whaling ships see a giant squid and live to tell the tale!"

Ahab quietly turned his boat back to the ship, the rest of us following. Queequeg had a different opinion about seeing the squid. "If you see a big squid, you see a big whale," he said.

CHAPTER 14

# A Catch

The next day was hot, making us all feel lazy and drowsy. Sure enough, as Queequeg said, we saw a large sperm whale floating off in the distance, spouting its jet like someone casually smoking his pipe in the afternoon. On seeing the whale, all signs of drowsiness vanished, and the men started lowering the boats. The noise we made must have scared the whale, for it threw its tail forty feet in the air and vanished underwater. When it resurfaced again, Stubb, closest to it, wanted the honor of capturing it.

Everyone began making various war cries. The men in Stubb's boat tugged and strained until the welcoming cry was heard.

"Tashtego! He's all yours!"

The harpoon whizzed by, piercing the whale. As the whale made a mad dash, the boat was pulled as well. It cut through the water like a fast shark, and when the whale finally slowed down, so did the boat.

"Haul in, haul in!" cried Stubb.

Using the rope around the harpoon, the men began to tug themselves and the boat toward the whale. Stubb shot darts, one after another, into the whale's body. Soon, a red tide flowed from the whale, tainting the waters around it. Looking at it, the men glowered at one another.

"Pull up!" shouted Stubb. The boat pulled alongside the whale. Stubb took out his long, sharp lance and slowly churned it into the whale's heart. The whale made one last desperate attempt to escape. Then the movement stopped, and the whale once more rolled out into view, opening and closing its spout

with sharp breaths. Streams of blood shot into the air and down the sides of the whale into the sea. The whale's heart had burst.

"The whale is dead, Mr. Stubb," said Tashtego.

Stubb took the pipe from his mouth and tapped out the last ashes. He stood thoughtfully and looked at the huge corpse he had just made.

CHAPTER 15

# Stubb's Supper

Stubb's whale had been killed a distance from the ship. Since the seas and weather were calm, we casually dragged the prize back to the ship. It took us a long, long time to tow the whale back to the ship. By the time we did, darkness fell upon us. Only three dim lights on the Pequod's main rigging guided us.

Vacantly eyeing the massive whale, Ahab gave the usual order of packing up for the night. He went to his cabin

and didn't come back out till morning. Captain Ahab, even though he had a dead whale on his ship, was not happy. The reason for this was that the dead whale was not Moby Dick.

Tied by the head to the stern and by the tail to the bows, the whale now lay close to the vessel. Floating side by side, the ship and the whale looked like two bullocks. Stubb, in a very good mood, ordered the whale to be made into a steak for dinner.

"I want a steak before I sleep. Daggoo! Go over and cut me a piece from the small of his back."

By midnight the steak had been cut and cooked. But Stubb wasn't the only one eating the whale that night. Below, in the waters, thousands and thousands of sharks began feasting on the whale. The smell of his blood had drawn them to him. A few of the men who slept below decks were woken up with a start as the sharks' tails hit the boat with a sharp thud just a few inches away from their hearts! Peeping over the side you could see them, swimming around the black waters, grabbing pieces of the whale that were as big as a man's head. It looked like the whale would be carved hollow by the time the sharks were done. Apart from the whale, they circled the ship hungrily looking at the men, like dogs

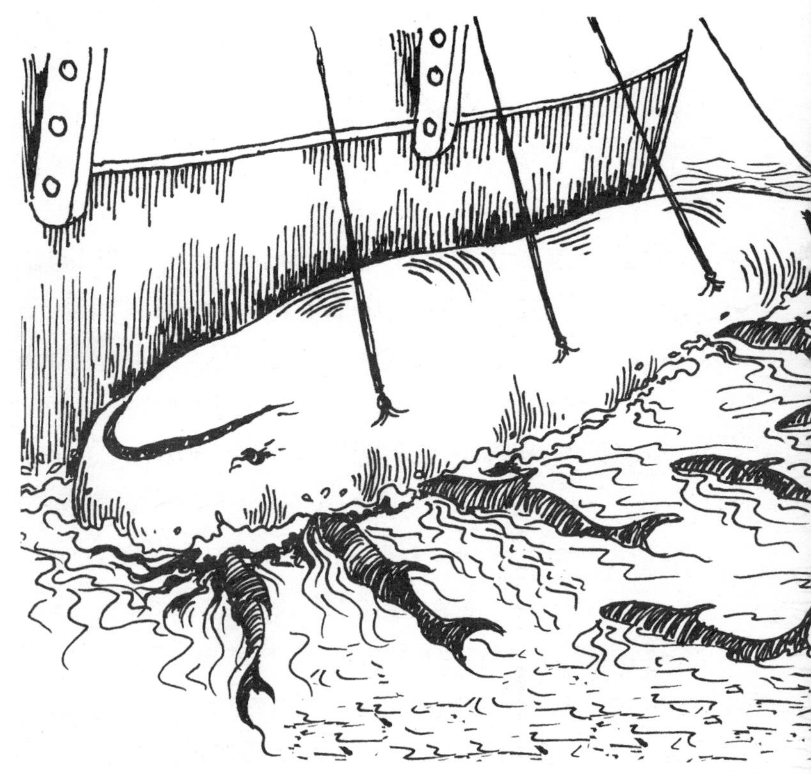

watching dinner being served. They were always waiting to pounce on and devour any man who was tossed overboard into their water.

Stubb ignored the mumbling at the dinner table and called out to the cook:

"Cook, don't you think this steak is a little overdone? It's too tender. Don't I always say that a whale steak must be tough? There are sharks feasting on the whale tonight as well. They prefer it tough and rare. What a commotion they are making! Go, Cook. Tell the sharks that they are allowed to join us for dinner only if they keep themselves in order. Preach to them. Take this lantern and off you go."

The old black cook scowled at Stubb, irritated to begin with at being woken up at this odd hour, and walked to the side of the deck. He took out the lantern and started in a loud voice:

"Fellow critters. You must stop making such noise! You hear? Stop smacking your lips so much! Master Stubb says you can eat your heart out, but stop making such a racket!"

Stubb rubbed his eyes and shook his head. "That isn't

# *Moby Dick*

how you preach to sinners, Cook."

"All right, then. You do it!" the old cook said, and turned to go.

"No, no. Please continue."

"Very well. Beloved fellow critters—"

"That's right. Just coax them a bit!" said Stubb.

"Even though all of you out there are sharks and very active by nature, I'd just like to say . . . that your activeness . . . oh, God! Would you stop that racket? How do you expect to hear me when you're thumping those tails of yours against the ship? Stop that right now!"

"Cook!" cried Stubb. "I'll have you talking to them like a gentleman!"

"Dear active critters. I don't blame you for your nature. It's who you are, and that can't be helped. You are sharks to begin with! Why should you be like angels? But what harm is there in trying to be civil? You can help yourselves to the whale, but please do try to be civil."

"Well done, Fleece!" cried Stubb. "That's Christianity. Go on!"

"It's no use telling them. They just keep bumping and scraping and scratching one another. They're just greedy pigs. They don't even hear a word that I tell them! The way they eat off the whale, one would only think that their stomachs are bottomless pits. Once they're really full, they'll definitely not hear you. They'll just go down the sea to the corals to sleep off them being full."

"Now, Cook," said Stubb, resuming his supper, "I want you to pay close attention. How old are you?"

"About ninety."

"You're telling me that you don't know how to cook a whale steak in the hundred years you've lived on this earth? Where were you born?"

"In a ferryboat that was on its way to Roanoke."

"You must go there and be born again and learn how to make this whale steak."

"Or I could make another one," the cook muttered, and turned to walk away.

"Cook, come back. Here. Try this steak and tell me how you like it."

Faintly smacking his withered lips over it for a moment, Fleece muttered, "Best steak ever cooked. Very, very juicy."

"Cook," said Stubb, squaring himself again, "do you belong to the church?"

"Passed one in Cape Town."

"And you have once in your life passed a holy church in Cape Town, where you doubtless overheard a holy parson preaching to his beloved fellow creatures his sermons, haven't you? Where do you expect to go to, Cook?"

"I expect to go to sleep," he mumbled.

"I meant when you die. I know, it's an awful question, but answer it."

"When an old black man dies, some blessed angel will come and fetch him."

"Fetch him? How? In a coach and four, as they fetched Elijah? And fetch him where?"

"Up there," said Fleece, holding his tongs straight over his head and keeping them there very solemnly.

"Don't you even know that the higher you climb, the colder it gets?" asked Stubb.

Fleece shrugged.

"You said 'up' yourself. Don't back down! I'm saying that your whale steak was very bad. The next time you make a steak for my private table, I'll warn you not to overdo it again and spoil the taste of it. Hold the steak in one hand and show it a live coal with the other; that done, dish it. You hear? And now tomorrow, Cook, when we are cutting into the fish, be sure you stand by to get the tips of his fins; have them put in a pickle. As for the ends of the flukes, have them soaked in brine, Cook. There now, you may go."

But Fleece had hardly got three paces off, when he was recalled.

"Cook, give me cutlets for supper tomorrow night in the mid-watch. Do you hear? Away you go."

"By God! I wish it was the whale eating him, not the other way around!" muttered the old cook as he limped away to his hammock.

## CHAPTER 16

# Cutting In

The next day, we began the long and hard job of cutting up the whale. A blanket of rubbery, thick skin covered the whale. In an hour, each and every sailor aboard the Pequod turned into a butcher.

And now, suspended in stages over the side, Starbuck and Stubb, the mates, armed with their long spades, began cutting a hole in the body of the whale for the insertion of a hook just above the nearest of the two side fins.

This done, a broad semicircular line was cut around the hole, the hook was inserted, and the main body of the crew struck up a wild chorus, and commenced heaving in one dense crowd at the windlass. Then instantly, the entire ship careened over on her side, creaking and groaning as the crow's nest bobbed and the long mast waved gently in the sky.

More and more she leaned toward the whale until a loud snap was heard. With a great swish, the ship rolled upward and backward from the whale. As the ship went back, the hook got pulled back, and the skin punctured by the hook was ripped off, like peeling the skin off an orange. As the blubber, in one strip, was peeled off along a line called "the scarf," it was cut at the same time by Stubb and Starbuck with their spades. The men at the windlass continued reeling the piece up until

its top portion grazed the rail of the ship. The men stopped pulling for a moment, taking in deep breaths. For one long minute, the blood-dripping mass swayed to and fro as if God was hanging it before us.

One of the harpooners moved toward the mass and, using a dangerous-looking weapon called a boarding sword, he cut into the lower part of the mass and sliced out a nice hole in it. Into this hole he put in another tackle. Then this accomplished, the swordsman warned us all to stand back.

Pulling back his sword, he went to cut up the mass completely. After making it ready for lowering, the crew members began their chorus again, and while one hook was hoisting up the piece, the other loosened it slowly. Then the piece went down into the blubber room.

In this dark room, various nimble hands coiled away the long piece as if it were a great live mass of interwoven serpents. And thus the work proceeded; the two tackles hoisting and lowering simultaneously, both whale and windlass heaving, the heavers singing, the blubber room gentlemen coiling, the mates scarfing, the ship straining, and all the men swearing occasionally, to relieve the general tension.

CHAPTER 17

# The Jeroboam's Prophet

Sometime later, we came across another ship called the Jeroboam. This ship came from Nantucket. When one of her lowered boats headed toward us, Starbuck ordered a ladder to be put down for the captain, who was coming to visit. But the commander of the Jeroboam waved his hand, saying that he wasn't coming on board the Pequod. It turned out that the Jeroboam had an infection running on board and that her captain, Mayhew, was afraid of infecting the crew of the Pequod.

Even though their vessels were quite a distance away from each other, this did nothing to hinder any form of communication. By carefully rowing the boat, the oarsman brought it alongside our ship, from where we could converse easily. The oarsman was a short young man with a freckled face and blond hair. There was a crazed look in his deep-set eyes.

Stubb seemed to recognize the man. "It's him! He's the one the Town-Ho's crew told us of!" Here, Stubb proceeded to tell us a strange tale of the Jeroboam and a certain crew member. Apparently, this man was looked upon as a soothsayer by everyone on his ship. Here's his story:

The fellow was raised among the society of the Niskayuna Shakers, where he had been a great prophet. On a strange impulse, he left Niskayuna for Nantucket. There, he managed to sign up as a sailor aboard the Jeroboam.

They took him on, but the moment the whaling ship lost sight of land, his insanity broke loose. He began announcing that he was the Archangel Gabriel, and he commanded the captain to jump overboard. With the earnestness in which he said these things—the daring play of his dark imagination, and a fear of delusion—the crew began to see him as sacred.

Moreover, they were afraid of him. As such a man, however, was not of much practical use on the ship, especially since he refused to work except when he pleased, the incredulous captain decided to land Gabriel in the first convenient port. Gabriel uttered terrible warnings of what would happen to the Jeroboam and her crew should the

captain put him off the ship.

The crew was so convinced by Gabriel's words that they ran to the captain and told him that should Gabriel be kicked off the ship, none of them would remain alive. The captain was outnumbered and was forced to forget his plan. The crew even treated Gabriel like royalty, giving him all the freedom in the world.

When the epidemic broke out on the Jeroboam, the men looked at Gabriel for help, giving him more power. He declared that the plague came about because he asked for it and he could make it go away when it pleased him. The sailors blindly believed everything he said. They began to worship him as a god.

That brings us to when Captain Mayhew of the Jeroboam and Gabriel rowed their boat to the Pequod.

"We don't fear your epidemic," said

Ahab. "Come aboard."

Now, Gabriel stood on his feet.

"Think of the fevers! Think of the horrible plague!"

Mayhew tried to say something, but a headlong wave came and pushed the boat ahead, cutting off the captain's speech. Ahab asked, "Have you seen the White Whale?"

Again, the boat tore ahead as if dragged by sharks. The waves were strong. The severed head of the sperm whale rocked violently, and Gabriel looked on in apprehension. Once all was calm, Mayhew began telling a tale of Moby Dick:

"A little while after the Jeroboam had set sail, the crew began talking of Moby Dick and of the havoc he made. The crew was very eager to hunt down such a whale until Gabriel stepped in. He warned the captain not to go chasing the whale. He called the White

Whale the Shaker God reincarnated. A year or two later, Moby Dick was sighted from the mastheads. Macey, the chief mate, desired to go after the whale. The captain didn't want to take away all the fun, for he himself was willing for a chase, in spite of Gabriel's warnings. Macey managed to convince five men to come with him on his boat. Gabriel rushed to the main masthead and began hurling prophecies of quick doom. As Macey and his men were poised with their lances for the kill, a broad white shadow rose from the sea. The next instant, the poor first mate was thrown into the air and flew across the sky in an arc, landing in the water some fifty yards away. Not a chip of the boat was harmed, not one hair on the head of the oarsman. But Macey was never seen again."

Having concluded his narration, Mayhew asked Ahab if he still wanted to go hunting after the White Whale.

"Yeah," came the reply.

Ahab remembered that he had a letter addressed to an officer aboard the Jeroboam in Nantucket. Starbuck arrived with the letter in hand. It was damp and mold had grown all over it. Starbuck took a long pole and attached the letter to it. As he reached the pole over the side and toward Mayhew, he tried to read the name of the person

addressed.

"Woman's handwriting. Mr. Har—Mr. Harry—hold on a second, Starbuck—Mr. Harry—Macey. Oh, Mr. Harry Macey. Blimey! It's your old chief mate! The one who died!"

"Poor fellow. It's from his wife, I bet. Let me have it."

"Keep it with you," screeched Gabriel. "You're going that way soon."

"Curse you to hell!" cried Ahab, outraged. "Mayhew, stand back to receive the letter."

But the letter managed to reach Gabriel's hand. He snatched it, seized the boat knife, impaled the letter on it and threw it back to the Pequod. It fell right at Ahab's feet. The boat then shot away from the Pequod and back to the Jeroboam, leaving Ahab and his men completely befuddled at what had just happened.

CHAPTER 18

# A Fiend On Board

Soon after the peculiar incident with Captain Mayhew and his "archangel," we came across a group of right whales. Now the oil you get from these whales is not as valuable as the one you get from sperm whales. So I naturally thought that we'd let them go ahead peacefully and not bother chasing after them. And naturally, I was quite wrong.

The cry came to the lower boats. Stubb and Flask went chasing after the tall spout. They got one whale harpooned as two boats came close to the whale. Stubb and Flask jumped on the whale and plunged their lances in and out until the whale was dead and ready for towing.

"I wonder what this man wants with this lump of old, foul lard," muttered Stubb.

"Wants with it?" said Flask as he tossed a spare line in the boat's bow. "Haven't you heard that if a ship has a sperm whale's head hoisted on the starboard and the head of a right whale on her larboard, she would never capsize?"

"Now where did you hear that rubbish?" asked Stubb.

"Fedallah said so himself!" said Flask. "I'm telling you, that ghost of a man will charm this ship to a bad end. Have you ever noticed that his singular tooth looks like the head of a snake?"

"Hah! Why would I look at him? But now that you mention it, I'll look at him when he ain't looking. Maybe in the night when he's looking over the bulwarks. You know, Flask, I think that this Fedallah character is the devil

in disguise. Do you believe that cock and bull story about him being stowed away on board a ship? He's the devil, I tell you."

Said Stubb vehemently, "Maybe we don't see his tail because he coils it up in his pocket. That turban covers up his horns, I'll warrant. He even sleeps in his boots! It's because he doesn't want us to see his cloven hoofs. I bet he even made a bargain with the old man, too. Got him to swap his soul for the giving up of

Moby Dick."

"You're joking now, Stubb. How could Fedallah do that?" demanded Flask.

"I don't know, Flask. But the devil is a strange and wicked old chap."

"How old do you think he is?"

"Lord knows, Flask."

"Look here, Stubb. I thought you were boasting a bit when you said that you'd toss Fedallah out into the sea if you got the chance. Now if he's really the devil, he must be ancient, and still living! If he ain't going to die at all, what's the use of throwing him into the sea?"

"We'll give him a good ducking, then. I'd like to see him try to do the same to me. Damn the devil! Do you think I'm afraid of him, Flask? If he makes even a little fuss, I'll reach into his pocket, grab his tail, and wrench it out! Then I'll graciously let him sneak off in shame."

"What will you do with the tail?"

"Do with it? Why, sell it for an ox whip when we get home—what else?"

Flask looked at Stubb, puzzled.

"Do you really mean what you've said about Fedallah?"

"What difference would it make, Flask? We've already reached the ship."

On the side of the ship, away from the sperm whale, there were chains hanging over the rail, ready to hoist the right whale up. The entire process that was followed in cutting up the sperm whale was followed for the other one as well. Soon, the right whale's head hung over the larboard. Meanwhile, Fedallah was calmly eyeing the head of the right whale, glancing from the deep wrinkles there, to the lines of his own hand. Ahab stood in such a way that he covered Fedallah with his shadow. It looked like Fedallah didn't have a shadow at all, but it seemed to lengthen and blend with Ahab's.

## CHAPTER 19

# Queequeg to the Rescue!

As the Pequod moved forward, a very important piece of work had to be done: the work of removing a treasure.

The "treasure" here was precious oil that comes from the head of a sperm whale. It is kept in an enormous sac called a case. When the head of a sperm whale is cut off, the cutter has to be extremely careful not to cut or puncture the case. If that happens, some five hundred gallons of oil would be lost. Tashtego climbed the main yardarm to the part projecting out over the swinging sperm whale's head. Securing himself to the yardarm, he lowered himself down with a rope. He climbed down slowly, hand after hand, until he landed on top of the whale's

head. One of the crewmen handed him a spade with a short handle. He first tapped the skin with the spade to sound its walls.

An iron bucket was lowered, like the kind that is lowered into wells. It was attached to one end of the rope. The other end was held by two men on deck who slowly lowered it down. Tashtego had found the perfect spot on the whale's head to cut by the time the bucket reached him. He rammed a pole into the bucket and thus lowered it into the whale's case until it disappeared. When the deckhand got his signal, they pulled the bucket up, which was filled to the brim with oil. On deck, it was emptied into a large tub and returned back to Tashtego. As the whale's case was emptied, the Indian had to ram the pole deeper and harder until finally, after about a hundred trips, it was some twenty feet down inside the whale's forehead.

Suddenly, Tashtego, who seemed to have lost his footing, fell into that very hole. With a horrible gurgling sound, he disappeared.

"Man overboard!" cried Daggoo. He put a foot into the bucket and shouted out to the deckhands to lower him down to the top of the head. Just then, a sharp cracking sound was heard. Everyone stopped and stared in horror. One of the two enormous hooks that held the head tore itself from the whale. The head hung sideways. The other hook, not able to bear the weight of the whale's head all by itself, began losing grip as well.

With a monstrous boom, the enormous mass fell into the sea. Daggoo clung helplessly to the dangling rope and watched in distress as poor Tashtego, buried alive in oil, sank to the bottom of the sea. The next second, a naked figure threw itself overboard from the bulwarks with a sword in hand. It was my good man, Queequeg, who dived perfectly into the gushing waters. In what was really moments, but seemed like hours, we finally saw an arm rising straight from the sea, like an arm coming up through the grass from its grave.

"Queequeg! He has Tashtego!" Daggoo shouted happily.

We all could now see Queequeg swimming toward the boat. He was

taking strokes with one hand and dragging Tashtego by his long hair with the other. When Queequeg described his rescue, we all thought that it was one amazing feat. He had gone down after the sinking whale's head and had poked holes around it with his sword. Upon reaching his hand in, he found Tashtego's leg. He grabbed it, knowing that this risked him being pulled in as well. After some quick thinking, he gave the leg a heavy toss. As he expected, Tashtego's body did a somersault inside the oil, now making it easier for Queequeg to make a grab for the head. He was then able to pull out Tashtego more firmly, and he swam back, pulling him along.

Now, had Tashtego perished inside the whale's head, it would have been a very heavy loss indeed. Hence, the crew was very grateful to Queequeg for saving Tashtego.

CHAPTER 20

# Trailing the White Whale

Ahab saw a passing ship with an English flag. He quickly got out his trumpet and spoke into it.

"Ship ahoy! Have you seen the White Whale?"

The captain of the ship, the Samuel Enderby, was a burly, good-natured, fine-looking man of about sixty. The empty right sleeve of his jacket streamed behind him.

"Have you seen the White Whale?" Ahab asked again.

"See this?" replied the captain. Holding up the right sleeve of his jacket, it fell aside to reveal a white arm made of sperm whale bone. The arm

ended with a wooden hammerhead. Ahab hobbled on his whale bone leg, shouting orders for a boat to be lowered. In a few moments, Ahab went aboard the Samuel Enderby. The captain of that ship looked at Ahab and his leg and beamed with joy. He extended his ivory arm and crossed it with Ahab's leg.

"Aye, aye, let's shake bones together—arm and leg. Was it the White Whale that did this, then?" asked Ahab.

"Aye, it was," replied the captain. "It was the first time in my life that I ever cruised on the line. I was ignorant of the White Whale at that time. Well, one day we lowered for a pod of four or five whales, and my boat fastened to one of them. Presently up breaches from the bottom of the sea a great whale, with a milky-white head and hump, all crow's feet and wrinkles."

"That's him!" cried Ahab. "That's

Moby Dick!"

"The whale had harpoons sticking in near his right side," said the captain.

"Aye, those are my harpoons! My irons! Please, go on, go on!" urged Ahab, a crazed look in his eye.

"He began snapping wildly at my boat and line!"

"He was trying to free himself. I know the devil. It's an old trick."

"The line got caught between his teeth, and when he pulled the line, our boat slid to the top of the hump! I'll tell you this, that was the noblest and biggest whale I've seen in all my life! So there, I resolved to capture him, in spite of the boiling rage he seemed to be in. I jumped into my mate's boat, grabbed the nearest harpoon, and let the whale have it."

"It was he, it was he!" cried Ahab, letting out his suspended breath.

"Next thing I know, his tail stuck up

out of the water and stood straight like a marble pillar. Suddenly, down comes the tail, cutting my boat in two, leaving each half in splinters; and tail first, the White Whale swam back through the wreck, as though it were just wood chips. We all struck out. To escape his terrible flailings, I seized hold of my harpoon pole sticking in him, and for a moment clung to that like a sucking fish."

"Well, what happened next?"

"A big wave knocked me off, and at the same instant, the whale, taking one good dart forward, went down like a flash; and the barb of that cursed second iron towing along near me caught me here at my shoulder and bore me down to hell's flames! All of a sudden, the barb ripped through the whole length of my arm and—and that gentleman there, Dr. Bunger, the ship's surgeon, will tell you the rest of the story."

Ahab stared at the point just below the shoulder where the captain's arm ended.

"At that moment, thank the Lord, the point tore its way along the length of my arm. It dislodged itself at my wrist, and I floated up."

The ship's doctor joined us and finished the story. "Aye, there was a two-foot wound. It festered down the entire length of his arm. It grew worse and worse. Eventually, we had to amputate it."

"But what became of the White Whale?" asked Ahab, for that was the only thing that really mattered to him.

"We saw him two more times," replied the captain of the Samuel Enderby.

"Were you able to catch him again?"

"Didn't even want to try. As if losing one arm wasn't enough! Wasn't going to risk losing anything else of me if I went after him!"

The Englishman looked meaningfully at Ahab's ivory limb. "I'm sure you would agree with me: Don't you think it's for the best to leave that whale alone? To stay out of its way?"

"Maybe, maybe not," replied Ahab. "But I'm still going after him. Tell me, which way was he heading?"

The captain looked shocked. "If I

rightly remember, he went east . . . I think."

He turned to Fedallah and whispered so that Ahab couldn't hear him, "Has your captain gone mad?"

But Fedallah just put a finger to his lips and slid over the Samuel Enderby's bulwarks to take our boat's oars. As soon as Ahab was standing in his boat, with his men springing to the oars, the English captain tried to call out to him, but in vain. With his back toward the Samuel Enderby, ramrod straight, he went back to the Pequod.

CHAPTER 21

# Back to Life

The cargo we were carrying was very precious. We carried barrels of whale oil, which was stored below decks in the hold. To see that the oil didn't spoil, our men went down there twice a week and hosed the barrels with water.

There were two reasons for this. First, the water kept the wooden lids of the barrels sealed tightly. Second, as the sailors checked the water that was pumped off, they could see if there was

*Moby Dick*

any oil mixed with it. That way they could see if there was any oil leaking from the barrels.

The morning after we met the English captain, our sailors were hosing the barrels as usual. That was when they realized that a lot of oil was rising and mixing with the water. Starbuck rushed to Ahab's cabin to report this.

"Captain Ahab, it is I. The oil in the hold is leaking, sir. We must bring the casks on deck and examine them."

Ahab turned around angrily from his table where he was studying charts.

"Now that we're nearing Japan, stay here for a week to fix a bunch of old barrels?"

"Either do that, sir, or waste in one day more oil than we may make in a year. What we have come twenty thousand miles to get is worth saving, sir."

"That's true," said Ahab, "provided we

are able to get it."

"I was speaking about the oil in the hold, sir. What will the owners say?"

"I don't care," said Ahab. "The

commander is the real owner, and I am the commander of the Pequod! My conscience is in this ship's keel. On deck!"

"But, sir," pleaded Starbuck, moving farther into the cabin.

Ahab was furious and turned on his chief mate with a gun in his hand.

"God rules over this earth, and Ahab rules over the Pequod! Now get on the deck!" he ordered Starbuck.

Starbuck, with his eyes flashing and cheeks burning, replied, "You have outraged, not insulted me, sir; but for that I warn you . . . beware of Starbuck! Let me tell you something—let Ahab beware of Ahab—you are your own worst enemy!"

So saying, the chief mate left the captain's cabin.

"You are too good a fellow, Starbuck," Ahab said in a soft voice. It was hard to know exactly why Ahab acted this way, since he respected Starbuck. It may have been a flash of honesty in him, but the captain realized that Starbuck was right, and it would be safer to keep as much good feeling as possible between the chief mate and himself. So he ordered the barrels to be checked for leakage.

All the harpooners lent a hand in the hold to check out the barrels. It was damp and hot in the hold. After battling with the whales in the water and then working in the hot, damp hold, Queequeg caught the chill and fever. He was so ill that he lay in his hammock in a very weak state, inching toward death. One day he made a strange request to his captain.

In Nantucket, there were wooden canoes available with lids, just like he had seen in his native land. He wanted his coffin to be made like this type of canoe. It would be like the custom his people followed in his native place, to put their dead in a canoe and let it float away.

The ship's carpenter was given orders. He took Queequeg's measurements

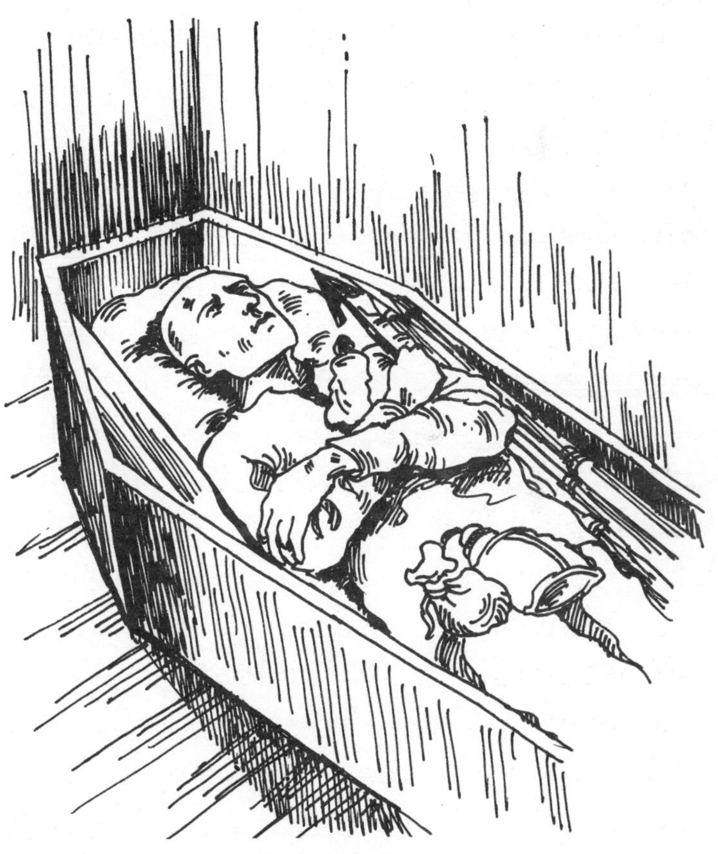

and started working on the coffin canoe. When it was ready, Queequeg tried it out by lying in it with his hands crossed and his little god Yojo on his chest. Later he asked to be helped back into the hammock.

After seeing his coffin, it seems he had changed his mind; Queequeg suddenly got better! Now, he started using his coffin as a sea chest to keep his things in, and he carved on the top of the coffin strange figures and drawings.

CHAPTER 22

# Strange Predictions

Captain Ahab also had a blacksmith called Perth on his ship. His job was to melt nails from the horseshoes and make really strong harpoons. While making one such harpoon, Perth asked for some water, which would cool or harden the sharp barb of the harpoon.

Captain Ahab had an idea. He wanted the barb to be tempered in human blood. So he asked his three harpooners, Tashtego, Queequeg,

and Daggoo, to offer their blood for the barb. They agreed, and soon their skin was punctured and their blood drawn to temper the barb of the White Whale's harpoon!

That night, Ahab had a nightmare in which he saw himself in a hearse. He went up to the deck to speak to

Fedallah who was keeping watch. Fedallah looked at the captain in the glow of a lantern and reminded him of his predictions about the captain's death. The captain would neither have a coffin nor a hearse. Fedallah also predicted that the captain would be seeing two hearses at the sea before his death—the first would be made by human hands, and the second would be made of wood grown in America. Yet another prediction that Fedallah made was that he would die before the captain and would reappear to guide the captain into the other world.

"Then I will be able to kill Moby Dick and live, too."

Fedallah also told the captain that only a rope could kill him.

"You mean by hanging? Ha! Ha! Ha! That's not going to happen. It means I will never die!" cried the captain.

Captain Ahab had guided his ship

toward the equator, for it was there that he had hoped to find Moby Dick. As they neared the equator, they heard strange sounds like wailing coming from an island. Some thought it was mermaids, while the others just kept quiet. The oldest sailor from the Isle of Man said it was the voices of the newly drowned men at sea.

When Flask mentioned the sounds to the captain, he laughed and said it was nothing but the cries of mother seals and baby seals. That was bad news, because most sailors are superstitious about seals, since their sounds seem like human cries and their heads look like human heads. Hence it was believed to be an evil omen and something bad was expected to happen.

And something bad did happen. The man keeping watch from the mainmast for Moby Dick fell into the water. He fell because he was half-asleep. He was

thrown a wooden buoy, but water got into it and pulled the man down with its weight.

The men were convinced that the bad omen had come because of the seals' cries. At that moment, Queequeg offered his coffin as a buoy. The officers thought it strange to use a coffin as a buoy, but they agreed and the carpenter was told to nail the lid tightly and to make the coffin waterproof.

A coffin had now become the Pequod's buoy.

The next day, the Pequod met another ship called the Rachel. Captain Ahab asked them whether they had seen the White Whale.

"Yes!" came the reply.

Captain Ahab was overjoyed. He wanted to go over to the Rachel to get some more information, but instead, the captain of the Rachel came on board the Pequod. The captain quickly recounted all that had happened when he saw the White Whale.

"Four of our boats went chasing after the white hump of that whale. Seeing how fast we were must have kicked in his speed! Our fastest boat had but then, him, suddenly, before I could even blink, both whale and boat disappeared. We searched all through the night, but we didn't see that whale or even the tiniest glimpse of my missing boat."

Ahab seemed disappointed, but the captain, even if he did notice it, continued. "I've come here to ask you to join us in the rescue search. Two ships can search much faster than one! We can go through the area in parallel lines in search of my missing men and . . ." He hesitated and then continued. "And my own son. He's among the men missing."

The captain looked at Ahab's cold expression and fumed. "For God's sake, man! I am begging you for your help! I want to hire your ship, and I will definitely and gladly pay you!"

"We must go and save the boy!" exclaimed Stubb.

Since there was a loud cry of approval from all the men on board, I figured that Stubb spoke for all of us.

But Ahab turned to the captain and spoke in a very calm and very cold voice. "I will not do it. We cannot afford to waste time, and that is precisely what is happening right now. I cannot help you. Good-bye and good luck to you."

The captain of the Rachel stood dumbfounded for a moment. His eyes bulged, and his jaw dropped in shock. Ahab turned to his first mate and called out to him:

"Mr. Starbuck, I want you to get these strangers off my boat in three minutes. Then get ready to sail once more."

CHAPTER 23

# The Pequod Meets the Delight

The Pequod ruthlessly went forth, cutting through the waves like a knife through butter. Many days rolled by. We soon came upon yet another ship, called the Delight, which in no way possible lived up to its name! As the ship drew close, we all fixed our gaze on her wide and broad beams, called shears, across the quarterdeck at the height of eight or nine feet. They were used to carry discarded and broken boats. There were many shattered ribs lying about and a few splintered planks of what had once been a whaling boat. Captain Ahab took out his trumpet as usual and spoke into it.

"Have you seen the White Whale?" demanded the hollow-cheeked man. "Have you had the luck to kill him?"

The captain of the other ship called back, "No harpoon has been made here that can do the job." He sadly looked around his dismal ship at the unusually quiet sailors sitting together, stitching up a hammock.

Ahab grabbed a harpoon and pointed it at the Delight. "Not made? Look here closely!" he cried. "In my hand, here, I hold the death of Moby Dick! It's been tempered by blood and tempered by lightning. I swear to temper it in the hot place behind that White Whale's fin, the place where it will hurt that monster the most!"

"Then God help you," said the other captain. "See there," he said, and pointed to the hammock where there lay a dead body, "one of five stout men from my ship died. Pity to know that he was alive just yesterday. Today, I bury him. He is the only one I bury. The others have been buried much before, but not by me. You now sail upon their graves."

The captain turned to his crew. "Are you ready, men? Right, then. Take the plank and place it on the rail. Lift the body so that we can—oh, God!" He advanced toward the rail with uplifted hands. "May the resurrection and the life . . ."

"Brace yourselves! Forward! Up helm!" cried Ahab almost instantly. But the Pequod was not quick enough to escape the sound of the splash as the dead sailor's body hit the sea. They

didn't move away from the hull quickly enough, and the water that splashed when the body hit the water sprinkled all over them just like a priest sprinkles water during Mass.

Ahab now walked away from the Delight and saw the strange coffin buoy on the stern of the Pequod.

CHAPTER 24

# The Chase—Day One

After the midnight watch that night, Ahab suddenly looked up sharply and sniffed the air, an eyebrow raised. He turned to us and declared, "There's a whale nearby."

Soon, all of us got the odor. It was the type that is made by sperm whales especially. Ahab quickly ordered that the ship's sails be shortened and that the course be altered slightly. By daybreak, all of us kept a keen eye on the waters for anything unusual.

Suddenly Daggoo screeched like a seagull, "There she blows! That's him with a white hump! Moby Dick, straight ahead!" Fired by his cry, the men rushed to the deck from the rigging to behold the infamous White Whale that they had pursued for so very long.

Ahab stood on his perch, a few feet above the other lookouts. Tashtego stood below him, and from where he stood, the whale looked to be about a mile away. His sparkling white hump was revealed with every movement of the waves, regularly jetting his silent spout in the air. To the others, the silent spout seemed like any other they'd seen on the Atlantic and Pacific oceans.

"Didn't any one of you see it before?" cried Ahab.

All the men ran toward Ahab, each claiming that the golden coin that Ahab had offered as reward was his.

"No!" cried Ahab. "The gold is mine! It was fate that made it appear only for me. I made Moby Dick appear!"

"There she blows!" cried Tashtego.

Ahab gave out orders excitedly. "Stand by! Get the boats ready." Saying so, he slid through the air and onto the deck.

Soon, all but Starbuck's boat were rushing headlong into the chase after Moby Dick. Ahab saw the wrinkles of the White Whale's head and the bright bubbles dancing playfully by his side. The broken pole of a whaler's lance still protruded out of the whale's back. In spite of that, he seemed calm and serene. The only thing about him that was frightful was his hideous jaw, which was hidden under water.

Suddenly, the whale rose up in a high, white arch. Then, he waved his long tail, almost as if shaking a finger in warning, and swiftly dipped below the surface of the whirling pool he had just left.

As the whirls subsided, the three boats waited for the White Whale to resurface. Ahab peered over his boat into the depths of the sea, but he couldn't see anything. Slowly his eyes widened as he saw a white object coming up toward the surface quickly. Once it was close enough to the surface, two long, crooked rows of white, sparkling teeth could be seen clearly. It was Moby Dick's mouth, wide open, looking like a white, wet burial chamber.

Ahab gave one sidelong sweep with his steering oar to whirl the boat around, away from the monstrous whale. This brought the bow of the boat around to face Moby Dick's head. But this whale turned out to be smarter than all of them, for he seemed to understand what Ahab had in mind while turning that boat.

He sneakily ducked under the boat and bumped the bottom of it with his head. His long, narrow jaw was now open. Soon, he had the bow in his mouth and one of his teeth caught in an oarlock. The inside of his jaw was just a couple of inches away from Ahab's head when Moby Dick began to gently shake the boat like a cat will do with a mouse in its jaw.

Fedallah sat calm and unafraid,

with his arms crossed, thoughtfully assessing the whale. The rest of the crew tumbled over one another to reach the stern, away from the whale's open jaws. Ahab, in a frenzy at being so close to getting his revenge but not being able to do so, grabbed the jawbone with his bare hands and tried to wrench it from its grip on the boat. But being slippery, the jaw slid from his grasp and came down on the boat like a massive pair of scissors, snapping the boat into two even pieces!

Everyone on board was thrown into the water. Moby Dick angrily circled the area, churning up the water. It was like he was readying himself for a deadlier attack.

The other boats hovered nearby, unharmed but still not daring to approach their fallen shipmates, fearing another attack by the whale. Luckily, the Pequod was able to sail

into the fray. Moby Dick swam off moodily and the other boats flew to the rescue. Half-blinded by the sea, Ahab was dragged into Stubb's boat.

"Get your hands off me!" he cried. "The blood is running hot through my veins again. Set the sail! Man the oars! We go after that whale!"

But even after the added rowing power of the crew members who were just rescued, the boat could not match the speed of the whale. And so, Moby Dick sped away.

When everybody was finally back on board, Ahab spoke again of the gold coin.

"That gold is mine," he said. "I've earned it. But it stays here until the White Whale is dead. If any one of you sees him first on the day that he is killed, this gold will go to you. If on that day I am the one to sight Moby Dick again, then that sum shall be divided among all of you ten times! Be gone now!"

Saying so, he took his position with his leg in the cutout on the deck and stood that way till dawn, sleeping and rousing himself. And here ends the first day of the hunt for Moby Dick.

CHAPTER 25

# The Chase—Day Two

The following day, there came a cry from the masthead above:

"There she blows! Straight ahead!"

Stubb gave out a joyous hoot, punching his fist in the air.

"Hah! I knew it! You can't get away. Blow and spit your spout, for I assure you it will be your last time doing so. The mad fiend will be on your tail himself. Let me tell you, he won't stop until he has drained every drop of blood from your body!"

The excitement of the chase spread like wildfire among the men. Any fear or foreboding they felt after yesterday's events was replaced by their growing admiration for the determination of their Captain Ahab. Thirty men worked as one toward the old captain's ultimate goal. Hardly had Ahab been hoisted to his high perch on the mast than a triumphant cry burst from thirty throats on board. Less than a mile away, Moby Dick came into view. He tossed his entire body out of the water and high into the air! This splashing was certainly an act of defiance.

"There she splashes!" came a shout.

"Moby Dick, reach out for your sun for the last time! Your time has come to get better acquainted with my harpoon! Men, into your boats!"

Ahab dropped down from his perch and onto the deck. "Lower away!" he cried as soon as he got into his boat.

As if to strike terror into them by being the first to attack, Moby Dick did a 180-degree turn and was now heading for the three whaleboats. This time, Ahab headed straight for the White Whale's forehead, because the animal sees better from the sides than from the front. But before they could reach him, and while all three boats were still within the whale's sight, Moby Dick churned himself into a furious speed. With open jaws and a lashing tail, he barged toward the boats. Ignoring the harpoons darting into him from all sides, he crossed and recrossed, getting all the lines tangled.

Caught and twisted in the mazes of the lines, harpoons, and lances, Moby Dick came flashing and dripping up to the bow of Ahab's boat. There was nothing left for the man to do but to cut off the line. As he did so, the White Whale made a sudden mad rush among the remaining tangled lines, thus pulling the boats toward one another, making them collide and overturn like roaring waves would do to two seashells. The whale then dived into the sea, disappearing in a boiling whirlpool. The two crews frantically circled in the waters, with Flask bobbing up and down like an empty bottle, twitching his legs upward to escape the dreaded jaws of the White Whale, while Stubb called out to be saved.

Ahab was about to go into the whirlpool headfirst to rescue those whom he could see when suddenly, his boat shot up from the sea. It moved as if being pulled by invisible strings from the sky. Moby Dick had dashed his broad forehead against the bottom of Ahab's boat and sent it spinning over and over in the air. Finally, it landed, upside down. Ahab and his men struggled to get out from under it.

Soon, as if satisfied with his work for the time being, the whale pushed his forehead through the ocean, trailing after him the intermingled lines. Just as before, the Pequod came to the rescue and dropped a boat for the floating crewmen, their oars, and their harpoons. Ahab was picked up

clinging to his boat's broken half. Thank God there were no deaths among the men. They only suffered bad cuts, and sprained shoulders, wrists, and ankles.

Back on the deck of the Pequod, Ahab half-hung onto Starbuck's shoulder. His ivory leg had been snapped off leaving a short, sharp splinter.

"Ahab is untouched!" he cried. "Not

even a broken bone. Here, man, give me that lance for a cane, and then gather the men together."

When the men gathered around him, Ahab searched for the face of only one man—Fedallah. But the man was not to be seen anywhere. "Where is Fedallah?" he demanded.

"Sir," started Stubb, "he was caught among the tangles of your line. I thought I saw him being dragged under."

"My line! My line? Gone? You know what this means, don't you? This is a sign of my upcoming death! It's a bad omen, it is. If I have to go around the globe ten times or even dive straight through it, I will slay Moby Dick yet!"

"Good God!" cried Starbuck. "You're barking mad! Old man, you will never capture him. No more. Enough of this madness! For two days you chased after him, for two days our boats were broken to splinters. Your very leg was snatched from under you. You've had enough warnings. Are we to chase this monster of a fish until he drags every last one of us to the bottom of the sea?"

"This is my destiny!" shouted Ahab. "This act was decreed by the gods a billion years before the oceans were born. Laugh, my men. They say that drowning things rise to the surface two times, then rise once more, only to sink forever. So with Moby Dick. Two days he has remained afloat. Tomorrow is the third day, his last day. Once more he'll rise, and then—and then I'll finish him!"

Then he said to himself, "Fedallah had predicted that he would go before me. But he said that I would see him once again before I died. Quite a riddle, that one. But it is one I intend to solve."

And so ended the second day's chase.

CHAPTER 26

# The Chase—The Final Day

The dawn of the third day was a fair one. Ahab, with a makeshift wooden leg, was hoisted up again to his mast in a rope basket. After an hour of searching the seas, he shouted, "There she blows! I meet you again, for the third time, forehead to forehead, Moby Dick!"

Patting the masthead lovingly, he said, "Good-bye, masthead. I'm going down now. You keep a good eye on the whale for me while I'm gone. We'll talk tomorrow, not tonight, when the White Whale lies down there, tied by head and tail."

As Ahab was being lowered, the riddle came to his thoughts again. He thought to himself, What was it that Fedallah said? He would go before I did, yet he would see me again. But, where? I've sailed far from where he sank. No, Fedallah, you may have been right in that prediction about yourself, but you are wrong about the one regarding me!

As Ahab climbed into his boat, he turned to Starbuck and stuck out his hand. "Shake hands with me, my good man. I am old, very very old."

Starbuck looked at Ahab, his eyes filling with tears. "Captain, I beg of you. Please don't go! I, a brave man, weep and beg you not to!"

Ahab wrenched his hand away from Starbuck's grasp and cried, "Lower

away!" The boats were lowered, but they had not gone far when a signal from the masthead, a downward pointing arm, told Ahab the whale had gone underwater.

As the waves rolled over and over on the bow of his boat, Ahab cried, "Beat on! Don't stop, men! I'm not afraid. I shall be there when Moby Dick rises again. Fedallah, you were wrong. There shall be no coffin and no hearse for me. Remember, only a rope can kill me! Ha-ha!"

All of a sudden, the waters around them swirled and swelled in broad circles. A low rumbling sound was immediately heard. The men held their breath as trailing ropes, harpoons, lances, and finally the White Whale shot up from the sea. Maddened by the day's fresh harpoons in him, Moby Dick came head-on, angrily churning his tail among the boats, spilling out the lances and harpoons and dashing part of their bows. As the whale turned and shot by them again, a cry went up. Tied to the whale's back, amid the tangled ropes, was the half-torn, bloodied body of Fedallah! His open eyes looked straight at old Ahab!

The harpoon dropped from the captain's hand, and he drew a long breath. "It's true, Fedallah. Your words have come true," he whispered. "I did see you again, after your death. And what you said about the hearse was right. It wasn't made by human hands, it was Moby Dick! But, where is the second hearse?" His eyes looked around frantically at the rest of his crew.

"Down, men!" he cried. "The first men to jump from this very boat will be harpooned by me. You are not other men; you are my men and my legs, so you will obey me! Now, where is that whale?" His eyes narrowed dangerously.

Moby Dick swam away from the boats at full speed out to sea. Ahab turned to follow. He was just passing the Pequod when Starbuck called down from the deck. "Ahab, it isn't too late for you to come back. Look! Moby Dick isn't after you! You are the one hounding him like a crazy fool."

Ignoring Starbuck, Ahab commanded his men to follow the whale. Glancing back to the ship, he saw Tashtego, Queequeg, and Daggoo climb eagerly onto the mastheads. He saw the oarsmen working on the two damaged boats that had been hoisted to the Pequod's side. As he sped past the portholes, he saw Stubb and Flask busy among the new bundle of irons and lances.

Ahab's oarsmen had trouble rowing. There were sharks gathered around their boat, making it difficult to move their oars. The sharks began biting at the oars.

"Don't pay them attention," warned Ahab. "Those teeth are only rowlocks for your oars. Forward, go!"

"But, sir! With every bite, the blade becomes smaller!"

"They will last long enough. Pull on!"

When they were alongside the White Whale's flank, the smoky mist from his spout curled around them. Ahab arched his body back and drove his harpoon deep into Moby Dick. The White Whale writhed and rolled his flank against the small boat, turning it partly over. Three of the men were tossed overboard into the sea, but Ahab clung to the raised side and remained inside the boat.

The whale then darted off into the sea. Ahab yelled at his men to hold the line fastened to Moby Dick. But the line could not withstand the strain, and it snapped!

As Moby Dick turned to face them, he spied the hull of the Pequod. He may have thought that the ship was the cause of all his trouble. He bore down on it with his jaws, ready to strike.

"The whale! The ship!" cried the poor cringing men.

"Move forward, men! Will you not save our ship!" cried Ahab frantically.

On board, the men were paralyzed with fear. They muttered and whispered prayers, and they stood transfixed, watching the White Whale charging toward them.

"Oh, Ahab," cried Starbuck. "Look at what you have done! The whale comes toward us now. God, stay with me now. That whale looks like he's ready to swallow us whole!"

Moby Dick's white forehead rammed the ship's starboard bow with vengeance. Men shook and fell flat on their faces as torrents of water started pouring through the break.

"The second hearse! It's my ship! My Pequod!" cried Ahab. "Its wood could only be American! That is what Fedallah said. A hearse made from American wood!"

Satisfied with the damage caused, the whale turned away from the sinking ship, dived beneath its keel, and came up quietly a few yards away from Ahab's boat. He lay there, still as a stone, for a while.

"You," growled Ahab, "you caused the death of my beloved ship. Oh my dear Pequod! Must you perish without me? Have you cut me off the pride of the captain? I shall avenge you. I shall fight that whale till my last breath!"

With all the power in him, Ahab hurled the harpoon. The stricken whale darted forward like a flash of lightning, tangling the harpoon's line with a jerk. As Ahab stopped to untangle it, a turn of the rope caught him around the neck, and he was flung out of the boat. Before the crew could realize what had happened, he was gone. Ahab was killed by a rope, as predicted.

For a moment, the crewmen stood still, as if they were in a trance. They slowly turned around. "The ship! Where's the ship?"

Through the mist they saw the Pequod fading into the sea, the faithful

harpooners still maintaining the lookouts on her high masts. Just then, a whirlpool of water seized the only remaining boat and spun it around until every member in it, lance, and harpoon was flung from it. Everything was carried to the bottom of the ocean. And the great White Whale sped away.

CHAPTER 27

# End of My Tale

Here ends my story. Needless to say, I alone survived the wreck. Let me quickly tell you how.

As I was being pulled around and around toward the center of the whirlpool, a coffin-shaped buoy burst from the bubbling waters and floated by my side. Even in death, my best and true friend Queequeg saved my life.

I floated on it the whole day. Surprisingly, the sharks didn't bother me. I had a lot to think about during

those hours that I floated alone in the sea. I thought of Ahab's ruthless drive unto death, and of the White Whale's fierceness. I smiled at my memory of Queequeg's kindness, and it boosted my spirits. How I shall miss him.

On the second day, a sail drew near and picked me up at last. It was the Rachel, which, in her search after her missing children, had found only another orphan.

# About the Author

Herman Melville was born on August 1, 1819, in New York City. His wish to become independent of his family's assistance led him to seek work. But this effort failed.

He later joined the U.S. Navy, and started his long voyages on ships, sailing both the Atlantic and the South Seas. In his mid-20s, Melville returned to his mother's house to write about his adventures.

Melville finally wrote his masterpiece, Moby Dick. However, it was largely misunderstood and as a result, it sold only 3,000 copies during Melville's lifetime. After an illness that lasted several months, Melville died at his home in New York City early on the morning of September 28, 1891. He was 72 years old.

# Treasury of Illustrated Classics™

Adventures of Huckleberry Finn
The Adventures of Tom Sawyer
Alice in Wonderland
Anne of Green Gables
Beauty and the Beast
Black Beauty
The Call of the Wild
A Christmas Carol
Frankenstein
Great Expectations
Journey to the Center of the Earth
The Jungle Book
King Arthur and the Knights of the Round Table
Little Women
Moby Dick
The Night Before Christmas and Other Holiday Tales
Oliver Twist
Peter Pan
Pinocchio
The Prince and the Pauper
Pygmalion
Robin Hood
The Secret Garden
The Time Machine
Treasure Island
White Fang
The Wind in the Willows
The Wizard of Oz